THIS ROOM IS IMPOSSIBLE TO EAT

NICOL HOCHHOLCZEROVÁ

TRANSLATED BY JULIA AND PETER SHERWOOD

Nicol Hochholczerová is an artist and writer.

THIS ROOM IS IMPOSSIBLE TO EAT

50

Someone is pulling out Ivan's hair, someone invisible. Ivan picks up the strands one by one, white hairs are difficult to spot on a white sheet, he throws them into a bin on top of some rotting fruit. He thinks of his daughter and how she used to smash to pieces the presents he'd given her, how he would pick up the broken bits one at a time and keep them in a drawer while she sat in her room, sobbing. He recalls how she sat there sobbing after Freddie Mercury died and Ivan held her in his arms until she fell asleep. He was glad that someone had died as it gave him a chance to be a good dad, he also felt glad at her mother's funeral as he could hold his only daughter in his arms, glad that she had come home for a few days at least, and after she left he had to fish out her hair from the bath plughole, and was glad again when the hair twisted itself around his fingers, he could barely peel it off and flush it down the toilet. What a shame that children, unlike strands of wet hair, peel off so easily.

Ivan lives in a cheap rented flat. During the day he teaches children to draw, and at night he dreams of the kind of music that used to make his daughter yell *turn it down, Dad*, and when he wakes up and turns his sweat-drenched pillow round, he finds watches ticking under it, an entire swarm of wristwatches slithering about like snakes. He really hates the ticking of watches and yet here they are, tick-tocking away right under his pillow; one curls up into a ball with a hiss, raising the end of its strap and letting an egg drop out. A child's watch hatches from it and starts ticking and wriggling about. *What the fuck*, Ivan swears, and flings the watches one after the other into the bin on top of the rotting fruit, but the pile doesn't get any smaller. In the end he climbs into the wardrobe and crouches on top of a heap of jeans, when he was young he could have killed for a pair of jeans, now he would kill for some peace and quiet, but the watches keep ticking, he can hear them even from inside the wardrobe, they seem to creep towards him as his hair is falling out and into his lap.

12

My room is impossible to eat. So are my fingernails, all I can do is bite them and cry when I come home from school because they called me an *ugly lesbo* for no reason, surely all girls practise kissing on girls, but it's worse when you're the only one who's ugly. They also call me a swot, but I don't have to study, ever, I just remember everything. My grandpa says I have too many brain cells for a girl, he actually treats me like a boy, making me guns and getting me used to eating stewed blood when we make blood sausages. Stewed blood is easier to eat than my room, it's also easier than eating myself, all of myself, from my cuticles right up to my ears, the kids at school say they are the size of dinner plates. I could write about this sort of stuff but I don't, because I entered a writing competition and we were told that it's not very original to write about being bullied at school, everybody writes about that, so I won't. And another thing one of the judges told me was: *I once read a book that began with the sentence, I got up in the morning and cut off my hands, that's exactly the effect your story had on me.*

I woke up in the morning and cut off my room but couldn't eat it up, and my last milk molar fell out and rolled under the bed. I got up in the morning and cut off my room, then I cut off the school; luckily my grandpa taught me to use an axe to chop wood, though it was only small chunks of wood with a small axe. But I couldn't eat the school either, only the vending machine spat out streams of melon and strawberry fruit strings, and Silvia came running out of the gym. Silvia is my only friend apart from Grandpa and Rumoš, she came and covered my head with her hands and looked daggers at the people who made me want to cut everything off, and then she looked daggers at me while chewing a melon fruit string.

Since Rumoš died, I don't have anyone who can stand my jabbering, even Silvia says *shut up and keep pedalling*. But Rumoš died a long time ago, first a card came from the sanatorium and then Grandpa slit the goat's throat because there was no one to look after it, as that used to be Rumoš' job. But his main job was to listen to me rabbiting on, everyone says *that Tereza never stops jabbering, she talks nineteen to the dozen,* and then they give me a hug.

But I remember everything because I have too many brain cells for a girl, only one day I will go quiet and won't say a word to anyone about anything.

My parents have made me take an after-school art class. I sit here chewing a pencil like it's my room, with heavy metal throbbing in my earbuds. I asked Silvia to take the class with me but she said no. So I sit here, not knowing a soul, and when I take my earbuds out, all I can hear is the scratching of pencils, the ticking of a clock and the jangling of keys and the sound of someone's steps, that would be you, my teacher. You're pacing up and down among us, jangling your keys and saying *what's that supposed to be, a horse, looks more like a rat, and is this meant to be a house, this wonky box?* I haven't drawn anything, there's a blank piece of paper before me and a pencil I can't eat up; you walk past and ask, *so what's this here*, you lean over my desk, your keys jangling, *a wall*, I say.

Then I start telling you: *I was one month old when I was baptised, I hadn't even grown any hair or teeth yet, and when the priest said, now let us pray, my grandma cried because I folded my hands like everyone else, what, how do I know that, I just remember; I also remember tumbling down the stairs, look, here's the scar; and I remember every fairytale I've ever watched, and I remember bawling when we couldn't go sledging because there wasn't enough snow, just like today, and I remember my mum leaving me out in the courtyard in my pram that winter to make me go to sleep, but by the time it finally started snowing she'd totally forgotten about me until my nose was the only thing sticking out from under the blanket of snow, that's when she stopped gazing at the snow and swooning, look at all that lovely snow, and dashed out to fetch me. And no, it wasn't my mum who told me this, it's just that I have an incredible memory, I never forget anything, and anyone who hurts me will be in trouble because I remember everything, I don't like that Hungarian saying – it's not your fault, someone has just cracked a whip over you – I hate it because I remember everything and if I cracked a whip over someone, I would fucking hit them,* and you laugh, you don't tell me off for saying fuck, you don't say watch your language, young lady.

Another time I sit here tossing a lump of clay from one hand to the other, it's going to be an ashtray, and I prattle away at the top of my voice to make everyone laugh but especially you, sir, *when I was little I was scared of brawn, there's this Hungarian fairy tale about a piece of brawn that lived alone in the attic and was so lonely that it ate up the whole village and then it kept rolling down the road with the whole village in its stomach until it swallowed a shepherd boy who slashed it open with a* bicska, *how do you say* bicska *in Slovak, oh yes, pen knife, and I was scared that something would eat me up too, that's why I've never liked brawn, my grandpa always laughs and says I don't know what tastes good, he says I'm sure not to have eaten anything better ever since there's been a hole in my arse. And he also says that when I grow up I should find myself a husband like Péter Esterházy, who's a writer and Grandpa says he's an actual count. So is his brother but he's a football player as well and Grandpa says that he likes football but all football players are dickheads as far as Grandpa is concerned, to be good enough for me Péter Esterházy's brother would have to play water polo. Grandpa also says my husband could be like Green Peter, you know the one from that Hungarian fairy tale, whose mother died and her head split open and a pigeon flew out of it, and he was the only one who could hide so well that the princess couldn't find him, even when she yelled: Green Peter! That's the kind of husband I'll have.*

And you say, *when I was little I was scared of pheasants, my father once came home with a pheasant, you know, it was for dinner he said, but it was still alive and started flapping around the kitchen and my mother chased after it, let me show you how to draw this, Tereza, first you do the bits that are for printing, take care you don't get it wrong, where was I, right, so my mum was chasing after the pheasant until it flew right out of the window. My dad flung my mother's jewellery after it, and when she asked what are we going to have for dinner, Dad said she should have thought of that earlier, then he went out, found her earrings under the window and said: here, eat that! In the end we had mushy beans, do you like mushy beans, Tereza?*

At home, I scrape the plaster off the wall with an earring and stuff myself with it like children with a mineral deficiency, but maybe they just want to know what the wall tastes like and what's behind it.

I go to your drawing class so I can rabbit away at you, because Silvia isn't in the class and can't tell me to *shut up and keep pedalling*, my parents aren't here either, with their *you never stop jabbering, can't you keep quiet just for a moment, just long enough to draw breath between two sentences?!* I chat to you about anything and everything, like this film I watched last night, the main character was a girl who made friends with a fox and the film ended with the fox leaping out of the window and falling on a bicycle which made a racket as the bell broke off. I also tell you about Rumoš because Rumoš was my best friend, I used to make him take dictation, and Rumoš always did what I told him even though he was Hungarian, honestly, don't laugh, he also showed me how to roll cigarettes in a little metal box and gave me rides on a goat, he used to hold the goat's head while I scrambled onto its back but I barely managed to straddle it before I had to tell Rumoš to take me off because the goat's back hurt me between the legs.

I'm telling you about this nature documentary I watched while Grandpa was asleep on the sofa. In this film wolves had climbed onto the roof of a cottage, knocked off a few tiles with their paws and snouts and took the roof apart to reach a woman who was asleep inside; first they chewed up her young breasts that spilled out of her nightie, then they chewed up her belly and pelvis, one of the wolves dragged her leg off into a corner and guzzled the toes, and when the animals were done with that, they got to work on the woman's head, the last thing they ate was her hair, which they spewed out in the forest later but spewing it out took them ages and they had to use their paws to pull it out of their snouts. That reminds me that at home we puke into this brown basin where we usually put dirty laundry, that's another thing I tell you about. And finally I tell you that I'm not sure if they really were wolves, because it was a long time ago and one of them actually looked more like a small fat dog than a wolf. But it still scares me, and I'm also scared of brawn and of sleeping in the shed. A week later Matúš, a boy in my class, makes a misshapen howling wolf out of clay and you crack up, point your finger at it and say, *look, it's a small fat dog!*

Silvia comes to pick me up with her new boyfriend, they're standing outside the school, smoking. As we leave, Silvia looks daggers at you, you look daggers at Silvia, I'm carrying a book and the CDs you've lent me, even though I don't have a CD player at home, instead I download the music from the internet and next day I tell you *thanks for the CDs, they're great,* and you say *it's one of my favourite bands but no one else likes them*, then I go over to Silvia, she's smoking outside the school gates and then pops a melon fruit string into her mouth to cover up the taste of the tobacco. When she's finished all the fruit strings, she folds the empty plastic bag and puts it in her school bag for later because that's what Silvia is like, she doesn't care about art but she cares about plastic bags and about me, that's why she always comes to pick me up and gives you the death stare.

The other day I showed you the scar from when I fell down the stairs and you rolled up your sleeve and showed me yours: much bigger than mine, it looks like something made out of dough. When I asked how you got it, you said *I was making love to a piece of glass*, I was going to raise my eyebrows but only my eyes popped out and you added, *I fucked it* and you laughed. That's when I knew that I didn't have to worry about saying fuck, although it shouldn't have bothered me in the first place because I listen to heavy metal, wear t-shirts with skulls on them and a chain on my jeans, and although I don't smoke like Silvia, I'm not a child anymore like when I made Rumoš give me rides on the goat.

You ask me what kind of college I want to go to. I say I don't know although I do, and you say I really should know by now, but I don't tell you that in fact I do know, not even when you show me a book on anatomy for artists and tell me to draw the woman on page forty-two. The woman on page forty-two has no hair, no breasts, no skin, it's as if she's been chewed up by wolves. I draw her muscles and think of my mum, who looks nothing like the woman on page forty-two, my mum's always tanned, she has blonde hair, a slender waist and slim legs, she likes to wear a red dress, but anyway, people always say I'm the spitting image of my dad!

All my clothes are black, I'm my parents' mini-funeral. You push your finger through a link in the chain hanging from my belt strap, *is this what kids are wearing these days*, I feel like snapping back, *no, they're fucking not,* but instead I lower my eyes and back at home I take the chain off, stuff it into a drawer and ring Silvia and ask her for a cigarette. Silvia comes over, laughs at me and then strokes my back while I'm choking on the smoke, *what's happened to that fucking thing you wear on your trousers*, I look daggers at her and before going to bed I clip the chain back on my belt.

You push your finger through a link in my chain and give it a tug, *get your stuff together, we're going to a concert, in a church.* You make my earring swing, the one with the upside-down cross that I use to eat my room, yesterday I tried to eat it again while my parents were screaming at each other, *fucking hell* and *sorry, darling, what are you mad about this time?*

Count me out, I say, but a few minutes later I'm there, sitting in the choir, holding the ashtray I made, I think I'll give it to Silvia.

In front of the church you say to me: *I love you!*

And in the classroom you tell me: *Forget about the 'sir', just call me Ivan.*

There's a cup of tea and a cake in front of you, you don't drink coffee because it gives you palpitations, you take me in your arms and say *so now we're on first name terms* and I nod, your name tastes like the plaster on the walls in my room, it scratches my throat but I keep swallowing it anyway, I'm proud that there's finally less and less of it.

Then you invite me over. When I get there, you open the door, you're wearing a jacket like you're about to go out, but we just sit in the kitchen, you make me a cup of tea even though I asked for coffee, but you say I'm too young for coffee, so I sit here sipping rosehip tea, looking around your room. I'd like to say something but I don't know what the hell to say, perhaps something about Rumoš or my grandpa or Silvia even though you don't like Silvia. In the end I point to the corner of the kitchen and say *my grandma has the exact same tiles in her loo.* You pinch my cheek and laugh, now I know I can really tell you anything, I can talk my head off non-stop.

As I put my shoes on, you ask if my parents won't be worried about me, *not really, I told them I'd be at Silvia's* I say, then I put my arms around you and hold you and hold you.

Back at home I hear something buzzing and sizzling in my room, it must be its blood stewing, I'll have to eat it.

It's still stewing as we sit in your kitchen, behind you are the tiles that are like the ones in my grandparents' loo, as well as an apron with your name on it. You're thumbing through a book called *From Rodin to Moore* wrapped in plastic; *and this statue here, it changed my life, I made one like that myself*, now you're the one who's jabbering away and I'm just listening, then at some point you stop and ask *can I give you a hug* as if you had never hugged me before; the other day you even gave me a smack on the bottom as I was leaving, I wanted to give you a kiss on the cheek but you didn't move your head and my lips landed on the corner of your mouth instead and now you're suddenly asking *can I give you a hug*, I've been in your arms for a long time waiting for you to turn your head and for the stewed blood to come gushing from your mouth.

Tereza is not his daughter, she could almost be but isn't, his daughter's hair is curly while Tereza's lies flat and lifeless around her face. His daughter has a pug nose while Tereza's is aquiline and she has thick eyebrows and lips that would look great with lipstick on, while his daughter's lips are a thin line, as narrow as the slot on a piggybank, too narrow for any of the little coins of his fatherhood to slip through, she would just throw them all on the floor and lock herself in her room. Tereza has a pair of lips that are kissing him now, letting his tongue slip between them like a gold coin, Ivan can hear the clinking of the coin, he can hear Tereza rubbing the gold coin on her thighs at home when her parents ask *where have you been*, and he can also hear Tereza reply *in town with Silvia*, her hands trembling throughout. They are trembling now as they clasp his face. Her hands are trembling as she caresses his back saying *don't cry, it's all right*, that's the kind of thing Tereza says to him and she also says *look, your hair is falling out, it's all over the place*, she picks up the strands and tosses them into the bin, wiping her hands afterwards.

13

You say, *we can be together but only for a short while, no one must know, but it's all right for a while.*

And also *we'll be together for ever and ever, I'll never stop loving you.*

And also *I didn't think you'd be so great at kissing!* You didn't think I'd be so great at kissing: I've been going around the school for days feeling proud of myself, pacing up and down and thinking only how great I am at kissing, how well Silvia taught me. You might find it interesting that it was Silvia who taught me, I'll tell you next time I see you. But it bothers me that you don't want us to kiss in front of the mirror, you don't want to watch the two of us together so we kiss sitting in an armchair surrounded by your statues, between a huge sphere with a pyramid at its centre, a statue called stairs into myself, and one that's a hammer beating a nail into its own handle, *it's a Christian hammer*, I say between kisses and you say, *you're such a smart little girl, so funny* and also *you're so great at kissing, it's been ages since I've had such a great time kissing anyone.*

I've been going to your place straight after school, I tell you how my dad crawled under my bed yelling that everything was covered in dust, *how can you live in this mess*, he yelled, and you stroke my head and say *I'd never say such a thing to my daughter, it would destroy my soul* and you also say *you remind me so much of my daughter, have you any idea how terrifying that is? really, no one must see us together.*

I've been going to your place straight after school, skipping lunch, at least I'll lose some weight. My grandpa says that if our country stood on legs as sturdy as mine, our lives would be a bed of roses, but I've no idea what you think of my legs. on my left there's a bruise from the bike and a mole with a single hair growing out of it, which I regularly pull out with my mum's tweezers. So I press myself against you, more with my right leg than the left, and you say *don't touch me like that, Tereza, d'you think I'm made of stone?*

My empty stomach aches a bit, the only thing I've eaten all day was half of Silvia's snack at break, she brought some fruit from home, straight from the freezer, still rock-hard. We continued to suck the fruit in class, hunched over our exercise books. We sat there sucking, saliva dribbling down our chins.

After school I slip my hand into your trousers for the first time. You remind me of a piece of brawn, neither hard nor soft, with a smooth surface that still gives off heat while the press mould is carefully tightened around it, juices dripping on the floor and Grandpa saying, *make it tighter* but Rumoš goes *better not, it might burst*, so that's what you remind me of but I'm not scared because I'm not a child anymore, I grin into your stubble as I slip my hand into your trousers, then I get down on all fours, to check that my dad is not under the bed.

Silvia lights up, the smoke merges with the perfume I've put on, it smells disgusting but it covers up your nice smell. *So what was it like*, she asks, she's found three grey hairs on my black jacket, she says I'd better stop wearing black, to be on the safe side, *nice,* I say as I shrug my shoulders and the ash from Silvia's cigarette lands there, gleaming just like your hair.

Like spending a long time sitting on the back of a goat.

52

Every morning Ivan texts his daughter, then he texts Tereza but only one of them ever writes back, never both. It would make him happier if it was his daughter but usually it's Tereza who replies, she ends her message with three hearts, three strands of hair stuck together. Today she wrote to tell him she's bought a pair of black stockings and borrowed a corset from Silvia, the image made Ivan laugh, the thought of the two girls struggling with the corset and tightening the laces, with one constantly coming loose. Except that one of the two girls is Tereza, wearing black stockings and a key hanging from her neck since he told her that it's the key to his heart. And it's Tereza who bursts into tears because she dreamt that he left her, and that makes Ivan burst into tears too, *I'd rather die*, and as he says that, he thinks of his daughter who has recently written to tell him she's coming home for Christmas after all. She will be wearing the slippers made shapeless by Tereza's feet, and washing her hair in the bathtub where he washed Tereza's hair, she tilted her head back and squealed when shampoo got into her eyes. And it occurred to him that the last time he'd washed someone else's hair it was his daughter's, who didn't say a word the whole time, and just stood in the bathtub with her arms crossed, letting the water and the shampoo stream down her face and wash the snot and saliva from her chin.

Ivan is happy every month when blood comes pouring out of Tereza. He bundles his little girl up in a blanket and kisses her on the lips; Ivan is happy every month when his daughter writes to tell him that the weather in Madrid is fine, that she has a great job in Madrid, that she's not dating anyone in Madrid and shares a flat with a gay couple and their tomcat. The first time Ivan feels jealous is when Tereza goes to Bulgaria on holiday, *the weather is nice and there's a waiter here who looks like you in your old photos, really just like you, darling, he has curly black hair and he's quite muscular, but not in a gross way.* Ivan sits in the kitchen smoking and can't be bothered to open the window and when Tereza comes back from holiday, he says *sweetheart, your hair is beautiful bleached by the sun like this, your eyelashes are beautiful bleached by the sun like this, and your skin is also beautiful from the sun, you have a lovely tan, like your mother, did you sunbathe naked as I told you to, you have brought the red dress haven't you, the one you're wearing in that photo, you have, good, you'll put it on as soon as we get to my house safely and without attracting too much attention, if you wore it now, sweetheart, you'd make everyone's head turn and everyone would wonder where this gorgeous woman comes from, so be a good girl now, sweetheart, go home so that no one sees us together, and next time don't forget to put on this dress, wear it tomorrow, you are coming tomorrow aren't you, I'll be waiting, just be careful, sweetheart, make sure no one sees you!*

4

I went home like a good girl and my mum stared at me and said *those legs of yours are quite a sight, you should stop stuffing yourself.* Back in my room I think of the gym class where we weren't allowed to wear knickers under our leotards and I think how my legs looked back then and how they look now when it's not my parents looking but it's you watching as I touch myself and you're saying I'm a gorgeous woman with gorgeous legs.

I touch myself picturing your body and your face, as it lies on a satin pillow, and worms come wriggling out of it, leaping out of your eyeballs and knocking on the coffin from the inside.

I came home like a good girl and Mum said *your room is too childish for you, what with that wallpaper and all that.* We get into the car and Dad cracks a joke, the kind of joke all dads crack and I laugh the way all daughters laugh, though Mum doesn't laugh, she says something cutting, my mum is Hungarian like Rumoš, *you should have thought of that earlier,* Dad snaps back and he pulls up in the middle of the road, he gets out of the car and walks off, I go after him and ask him to come back, he knows full well that Mum can't drive, but he says we should have thought of that earlier, lumping us neatly together in the plural as he marches on, I go back to get Mum but she's gone, all I find is the empty Alfa Romeo, its number plate askew, attached to the left-hand side of the bumper, *Dad, this car is hideous,* I said when he first brought it home and I was right, I still think it's hideous.

I'm scared to go home so I go to your place, you bundle me up in a blanket and give me a slice of bread and butter, *here, eat this, sweetheart, sadness is just hunger in disguise.*

But my mum was gone, don't you get it?

I know, you say, and kiss me the way sardines kiss the inside of their tin, you're all crammed inside me. No one is missing me and you keep saying, *I know just how you feel.*

You tie my hands with the chain from my trousers; we're my parents' mini-funeral.

But they should have thought of that earlier.

Then, back at home, I touch myself and I'm happy that no one has found out, no one was looking for me, I went over to your place and returned home like nothing happened and found my parents sitting on the sofa like nothing happened, my dad in the middle and Mum asymetrically on the left, they're askew like that hideous number plate, they don't say a word, although they might know everything, but I guess we should have thought of that earlier.

When I come home, I try to ring you but you're not picking up, you haven't picked up for days, my room is stuffing itself into my mouth by itself.

Please don't cry, sweetheart, it breaks my heart to see you cry, I've said I'm sorry, so please stop crying now, come on, stop that bawling, why don't you go for a walk instead, go to the woods, climb the highest hill, find the most beautiful pine tree and chop it down, that will tire you out nicely and stop you crying, and have something to eat because sadness is just hunger in disguise, and once you're up on the hill you might as well go sledging, you could also carry the pine tree down on the sledge and set it up at home, oh but you've left the sledge at home, see, you're already laughing, there's a good girl, go on, laugh, sweetheart, it's quite funny isn't it, so many silly things in a day, not only have you left the sledge at home, you've also chopped down a pine tree for no reason, haven't you, see, you're laughing now, sweetheart, that's better, just don't cry, it breaks my heart to see you cry!

You hold me in your arms for a long, long time, you stroke and comb my hair, you put cream on my face, all red from your stubble. Then you say *you're just as beautiful as your mother!*

You say:
> *Your lips swell up after orgasm.*
> *Your cheeks swell up after orgasm.*
> *Your thighs stop being swollen after orgasm, your legs are gorgeous and slim.*

Sledge right into me, that's quite funny, isn't it?

But sweetheart, you really turn me on, I'll come straight away! Surely you don't want to get pregnant, do you, sweetheart?

Your little bum is so cute, sweetheart, you have the loveliest bum in the world, but that heat rash, you should do something about it, put some witch-hazel on it, or camomile, or some other anti-inflammatory, your rash will be gone in no time and you'll be just perfect, the most gorgeous girl on the planet.

The handle has to be glued on properly, sweetheart, like this, see?

At school you call everyone sweetheart but I'm the only one you kiss in the storeroom after class, when we're there I don't dare move for fear of knocking over some of the jugs and plates and clay animals on the shelves. I lean on you, *just be careful, sweetheart, watch out for those jugs, see how sloppily the kids have glued the handles on, they stick out like ears, they're bound to break off in the kiln; and look how these stupid animals have been cobbled together, though this giraffe is cute, look at it, sticking out its tongue!*

I stick out my tongue, but carefully, for fear of breaking something.

On Sunday I say to my parents I'm going for a walk. I tell a lie for fear of breaking something. We sit in your flat, you stick out your tongue into me, slicing fruit with it.

You know, when my daughter got up in the morning her hair was sticking out all over the place!

You know, my wife, she never loved me, she would never hold hands with me out in the street.

My parents used to fight all the time, so I would run to my grandma's house and build mud castles in her courtyard.

I stick my tongue into your crotch to cheer you up. So you stroke my hair and then it lies flat and sticks to my head.

Tereza, sweetheart, do you have any cash on you? Be a good girl and get us some beer.

So I go even though I'm scared that someone might see me, I was already scared on my way over and now I have to be scared again, but I know you will comfort me when I get back, I could see in your eyes that you'd do anything you could see in mine, so off I go to the shop, but the lady behind the counter is the one from whom Rumoš used to buy tobacco for himself and fruit strings for me. She's bound to know that she's not allowed to sell me beer so I ask for a fruit string and dash back to your place. I leave my cried-out eyes all over you, like freshly plucked plums in a bowl.

I go to the market to buy fresh strawberries, fresh raspberries, fresh sour cherries; you suck off their flesh and spit the stones into my body. Fresh fruit has to be really, really fresh, no streaks on the skin of the legs and no stretch marks, like the fresh ones that were there when I took my knickers off. It's supposed to be normal while you're growing. But breasts mustn't be soft like plums, they must be firmer and always fresh, unlike your body.

I told my parents I'm going for a walk. Instead, I'm sitting by your side and while I wait for you to touch me, I watch a fruit fly flutter around the full bowl. It lands on the sole of your foot, crawls in, its little black head drilling down and buzzing while it's trying to force its body into all that flesh. It disappears from sight for a moment but then I feel it buzzing inside my own foot. It crawls out of my foot and flies off into the kitchen, where it circles the rubbish bin.

I'm waiting for you to touch me, I wait and I will keep waiting, meanwhile I get home and my dad says *it's because you're too impatient, you can't expect everything to always be just the way you like it!*

But you, darling, you behave just the way I like it, you let your hair grow just the way I like it, you dress just the way I like it, you undress just the way I like it, you press your lips on my pussy just the way I like it.

You put your arms around me in front of my father.
  Your daughter is very special!

You get my favourite dish for lunch, that too is just the way I like it, we eat from the same plate, using one spoon, one hand, and one mouth. You're kissing me with the other hand under the table and when I offer you some leftover meat you cover me in kisses again and say, *eat some more, sweetheart, you're still growing.*

You've eaten my eyes, now I can't see how old you are.

You've eaten my hands, now I can't feel how soft you are.

You've eaten my father, who doesn't yet know what you're like.

Eat some more of me, darling, I say, and you bite into my sticky-out ears.

Take another bite of me, darling, I said, so you come to the rehearsal for our first school ball for that bite. You said you wanted to see me in a skirt and heels, so here I am. And so are you, during the break we're holed up under the stairs by the loos and you say *wear these heels tomorrow when you come over*; a classmate comes running down the stairs and as she catches sight of us kissing through the railing, she wets herself on the spot, instead of tears a trickle of her urine flows down my cheek.

Because there are many different ways of giving ourselves away!

But we should have thought of that earlier.

Now I sit here crying, but I should have thought of that earlier, I should have thought that one day I would cry, in fact I did think of it and now it's happened. Mum is sitting by my side saying, *he's no good for you, he's no use to anyone anymore, just forget about him.*

But I remember everything, even my own baptism, and how Rumoš gave me rides on the goat, and the gristly bits of brawn that were impossible to eat, which Grandpa used to push to the side of his plate; and now my memory will go all damp like this, wrapped in clingfilm, with the chain from my trousers wound around me like this. Anyone will be able to poke their finger through my memory like through a link on the chain that looks like an eye, like a human eye, all soft and sticky.

But Mummy, eyes like these will be no use to anyone!

53

When he wakes up and turns over his sweat-soaked pillow, there in a little puddle of sweat is Tereza strolling around. She's strolling around a miniature version of his apartment block waiting for the right moment to ring the bell so that no one sees her, but although she manages to ring the bell, there's no answer, she rings again but again nothing happens, Tereza sits down on the kerb and sits there crying for a while, Ivan can clearly see that she's not wearing knickers under her dress. As he looks at her, he thinks that hidden under his pillow she looks exactly like the statuette he carved fifteen years ago, he'd drilled a hole into the middle of a wooden stick, attaching it to a small mount. The statue was minuscule, barely three centimetres tall, but even so, you could look out onto the world through its tiny hole. This is what the statuette he made fifteen years ago was like, he would carry it everywhere in a hand-made box, three-and-a-half centimetres in size, *look at this thing I've made,* he would tell everyone, and everyone was amazed, *it's exactly like your other ones only incredibly tiny, who would have thought you have such delicate hands, such a delicate touch, is it really not machine-made?* And now, fifteen years later, there's Tereza under his pillow, crying, she's exactly the same as the real Tereza but this one is incredibly tiny as she sits there on his sweat-soaked sheet sobbing into her hands while Ivan is telling her *are you listening to me, Tereza, I told you we couldn't go on like this, I can't take it any more, do you hear me?*

15

My room is impossible to eat. I can't chew it noisily and then prise what's left from between my teeth with the tip of my tongue, it's impossible to turn it inside out and patch it up, my room can't bend down and stick out its bum so that its head can be cut off while I sit here in this room of mine, where there's nothing I can do. I suppose I could leave it, but what for, if not to see you? The only point of leaving my room would be to go and see you, but that's not allowed anymore; the only thing that's allowed is to go cycling with my dad, riding down the high street, with cars everywhere. Being on the road feels better than being stuck inside this room, where people keep peering in all the time. But then it feels bad again so I take off my helmet, sit down by the side of the road and cry. Dad stands over me drinking water, chewing it noisily, even after we get home he keeps prising what's left from between his teeth, even at home he keeps prising me from between his teeth but he can't manage it.

Maybe it's because I'm not actually between his teeth but in my room, and this thought makes me laugh, aren't I a witty girl?!

Meanwhile in the kitchen Dad is on his knees, crying, his head is all slimy from his tears.

I'm combing my long hair but the comb isn't your hand; I throw it away along with the hair. Later I see you standing at your closed window and pointing to where my plaits used to be, I can't hear what you say as I'm still not allowed to go in and see you so I shrug my shoulders and run home, halfway there I sit down by the side of the road.

You're a strand of hair down my dad's throat.

I don't have my own room in your flat, I don't even have the keys, your flat is entirely yours, but I'm all yours too, so where does that leave us? Even after a long absence I feel at home in your flat, I look around to check what's new, you've changed the tiles in your kitchen.
Where's your hair gone?
My hair?

I'm so happy to have you back.
  I'm so happy, I was going out of my mind.
  I'm so happy, I'll never let you go again.

My dad has no idea that again there's a strand of hair down his throat, or he's forgotten, he's wolfing down his dinner happily, chewing noisily and licking his fingers.

Yesterday you put your finger inside my mouth and said *I'm so happy that you're thinking about it all the time as well!*

I love looking at you while we're doing it!

I will put it in you all the way and watch your face as I'm doing it, Tereza.

I will put it in you from behind and as I do, I'll tell you how sensible and grown-up you are.

A blister has appeared on my finger. I pierce it with a red-hot needle, my hands trembling, I dip the wound in camomile infusion but the liquid isn't me because you've never dipped anything in me all the way, you only keep talking about it, but you're very careful and when I pull my finger out of the infusion, the old skin comes off together with the blister, leaving fresh skin that's sore.

The camomile infusion was Silvia's idea, my skinless finger makes her laugh as she shares her latest news, about her brother who has started to keep bees and make honey, how you must use a clean spoon to scoop up the honey or it will go hard, how you mustn't dip the spoon first in honey, then in tea and then again in honey, only people who don't know shit about honey do that. Silvia's brother says people like that might as well stuff themselves with white sugar and drop dead from a heart attack. Silvia makes fun of her brother, too.

I kiss your thighs and say *I am the honey and you are the clean spoon that loves me.*

When I ask you what you'd like to eat, you say *you!*

And when I ask you what's going on, why you're frowning, you say *I should never have got involved with that woman! Even my daughter preferred her to me, they were combing each other's hair all the time.*

Last week was the first time I stayed at yours overnight. As soon as my parents cleared off, left town and the country and crossed the border which is impossible to eat or chew. The minute they crossed the border I was over at yours, with no knickers and a bottle of wine, first you spent hours telling me what you would do to me, then you did it to me and then you fell asleep, *I feel so safe when you're with me, Tereza*, I stayed up all night, staring at the door of your wardrobe and when you woke up, you said *I'll put my finger between your lovely lips and that's how I'll fuck you,* and then you put your finger in my mouth and said, *You're the one I've been waiting for all my life!*

54

Ivan wakes to find Tereza sitting up in bed next to him, she's dozing and there are little folds on her belly. He'd like to tell her that she'd be better off with a boy her own age, that's the sort of person she needs, not Ivan who's been trying to teach her how to skin a chicken so that the skin stays in one piece. He slipped his fingers under it and began to slowly peel it away from the flesh, it ended up dangling from his hands like a wet rag, with the odd unplucked feather here and there. Then he broke the thighs out of the joints, ripped off the wings and separated the breast and wrapped the bones and what was left of the meat in clingfilm and stuffed it into the freezer while Tereza sat there gawping, just as she is now, opening her eyes wide as if she hadn't slept at all, no gradual awakening or yawning, just some saliva in the corner of her mouth. She asks if he will leave her if she goes to college in another town, because that's what she's really scared of, she really doesn't want to burden him with this but she had to ask, she'd been asking him the whole time he was sleeping but he never answered and now he shakes his head, *of course I won't, I told you you're the one I've been waiting for all my life!*

16

Silvia asks if I'm not afraid of moving to another town and I tell her I'm not afraid of anything. We're working on our tan in the August sun, Silvia's superslim legs and my sturdy pillars dangling from the balcony.

Then you ring and say, *Tereza.*

Just leave me alone, stop ringing me, and don't even think of coming over. My daughter is visiting and she's got a whiff of something so get off my back, I've had it, I'm sick and tired of this.

Silvia asks if everything's okay, presses another cigarette into my hand and says, *listen, he'll come back to you, he's just playing up as usual, fuck, I should have put on SPF 30, my legs are stinging like hell.*

Silvia smokes Marlboro Reds, because that's what her brother smokes. And that's what I buy on my way to college, the girl at the station kiosk can't be bothered to ask for ID and I look like a woman now, everyone says that, including you. The queue behind me is getting longer, all these people are on their way to see someone, I'm on my way to see you, or sometimes some boy. With a cigarette, in this town where I don't know anyone, only Silvia rings every night from Košice, where she's at college now, and asks *how's it going, it's really boring here, they keep tabs on us, like all the time, to make sure no one is smoking by the window, we have to go to the loos for a smoke.*

The limbs of one of the boys looked like the twigs of a dead redcurrant bush; when he puts soap on his prick, it makes his arse froth up, as Rumoš would say, not to me, only to Grandpa in a stage whisper.

This boy's spine was as sharp as a goat's.

He never once put his elbows down on the table while eating, I keep watching and waiting for him to put those elbows down, but he never does, and I hate waiting.

I rang you once on my way to see a boy like that and you said, *but it's me that you love, Tereza.*

I hate the way this boy eats, I hate this restaurant, the food here tastes like shit, and yet they put this fancy napkin swan on my plate which I have to remove before I can eat from it. The boy's name is Martin, what sort of name is that, that's what every boy is called and none of them will put their elbows on the table while they eat. Speaking of you, this boy said *I don't understand how he could have dumped you.*

I'm in the station restaurant with Martin, he asks all sorts of questions but won't put his fucking elbows down. There's a couple sitting to our right, both have their elbows on the table so they can hold hands, the woman lets go of the man's hand only for as long as it takes her to remove the spine from her roast trout, and that trout is you, you are staring at me with your eyes all breadcrumbs and saying, *but it's me that you love, Tereza.*

Martin reaches out to me, he takes my hand, now, I think, he's surely going to put his elbow down!

But instead Martin lifts my hand to his lips and kisses it, his kiss tastes like a wholemeal roll that's supposed to be good for you, so I let Martin hold my hand above the tablecloth, the plates, the spoons, forks and knives; *I don't understand,* Martin says, *how he could have dumped you*, and he's right, how could you? When Martin lets go of my hand, I pick up my spoon and take some soup, describing an arc over the fork, the knife and the napkin swan, and put the spoon into my mouth.

I could stick it further down my throat, all the way down, that's not a problem for me, I could swallow it all and the spoon would slide down my throat, right down into my stomach and then keep sliding further and further down until it would slip out of me, but rather than a spoon it would be the son you always wanted, *Tereza, when I'm born again, you'll be the one to give birth to me.* Instead I'm sitting here now, waiting for Martin to put his elbows down on the table but all he says is *I don't understand how he could have dumped you.*

You can't dip your soup spoon into boys like that, or prop your elbows on them, as that would make boys like that break, they would snap like a dead redcurrant bush, that's what I keep telling myself before I go to sleep.

Jerguš sits down in the pub opposite me, puts his elbows down on the table, folds his hands together like a proper philosopher, props his chin on them and says, *what's up?*

He's the one I'll give what's left of my virginity.

Hey, do you want to take what's left of my virginity?

Oh, not much.

Jerguš is self-conscious when naked because of his caved-in chest. Like a lake you can weep into. Like a hilltop that has changed its mind and decided after all to keep what's left of its virginity to itself.

Jerguš' fair hair falls onto his shoulders.

We were only ten the first time we met, he touched my flat stomach, and his brother and Silvia shouted, *go on, give her a kiss!*

Then there's Dori Frolov; Dori Florov comes from Ukraine. He claims I look like a Portuguese girl and that my eyes are more beautiful than the roofs of Slovakia, because whichever town he's in, it's the roofs he loves to look at. Then he mentions that he writes poetry. He has some important date tattooed on his arm, his mum's birthday or his dad's birthday, my birthday, that sort of thing. I lick the tattoos, they taste like a sell-by date, like adolescent poetry translated from Ukrainian.

Then there's Ringo, no idea what his real name is. He says, *you're the sexiest dancer ever,* and *your eyes are the most beautiful ever,* he also says *my name is Ringo because I make every woman's heart ring like a bell,* because in Slovak, the clapper of a bell is called its heart, and Ringo whispers into my ear *your brain is the smartest ever!* I phone you in the morning, I'm sure you know what I've been up to, I'm sure it hurts you, now there's really no reason for you to take my calls because my heart went ding-dong for a moment, but never mind, it was only my heart, and anyway, Silvia would say *who gives a shit,* and the judges at the writing competition would say *another cheesy cliché, unlike the woman who got up and cut off her hands,* and my dad would say, *I'm beginning to doubt that you're my daughter.*

You say, *I'm so glad you rang, sweetheart, I just love the sound of your voice, and whenever you come to see me you look radiant, I'm so glad to see you happy, I'm so proud of you!*

In the morning I fish a strand of hair out of my mouth, it's yours, it's long and grey, and there's a spoon tied to its end.

Maroš manages to catch the bottle of wine with one hand that's still sticky, before the bottle tips over into the grass, while zipping his trousers up with the other. I check my phone; a message from you has flashed up. *It's been a while since you sent me a tiny short story.* Next day I dash to the post office, a tiny envelope under my arm, a tiny short story in the tiny envelope; *what is this about,* the judges asked, *is it just that she's into older men, or is there more to it?* Everyone laughed and I pulled a face. So the story I'm sending you is this old one, as I don't have anything new, and while you're reading it, I'll ring Maroš and ask if he wants to go out for a drink.

The next day you say *my sweet little Hemingway, your writing is so amazing that no one can understand it!*

But in fact I don't write anymore, I just spread my legs.

I don't write anymore, I just spread my legs, I sit straddling the bench and drinking, with people all around me who aren't you or Silvia. They scoff crisps with their beer because they don't actually like the taste of it, they break up right here, live, and then they make up and kiss right here, they order another beer and discuss projects and music that feels fresh and crisp, a few months old rather than decades. I sit among them reading, and Anita asks *what're you reading*, knocking back her beer as if she enjoyed it, Anita is beautiful.

My teachers are beautiful too, their beards are beautiful, and their bums in their tight trousers are beautiful, there's always some body part or other that's in a cast or at least a splint or elastic bandage, even my teacher of Slovak is beautiful when she asks if I might need a psychologist, *if you need a psychologist, Tereza, I can give you the number of the one my sister used to see, he was brilliant*, but I shake my head. You used to be jealous of these people. Now I ring you and tell you how beautiful and smart they are but you interrupt me saying *I'm at my girlfriend's laying floorboards, call back later.*

I ring back later and you say:
> *I can't live without you.*
> *I can't get you out of my head.*
> *I can't get enough of your body.*

You lean me against the kiln filled with jugs, plates and clay animals; even through my clothes I can feel it burning my back. The next day you show your girlfriend the vase she's made, shouting triumphantly *this glaze has turned out beautiful, Magda my dear!*

That beautiful glaze is my blood.

Silvia and I go out for a beer; she's rocking her chair while I tell her about Oliver *he's so hot, he's really fit, but you know what he said to me, he said that writing is easy, because, like, you don't need anything for it, but you can't take a piano wherever you go, do I have any idea how long he had to practise his scales, no I have no fucking idea, but anyway he's really hot,* Silvia shares a sigh with me and listens attentively. *And that old dumbass,* I tell her with the lips that blow boys who are actually quite hot, *that old dumbass hadn't been in touch again for a whole week, but you should have seen him crawling back to me later,* and when I ask Silvia how her week went, which I never do, because that's not the way it goes, I just sit there a bit longer, slowly sipping my beer to indicate I'm done and it's her turn, Silvia keeps rocking her chair and says, *oh you know, nothing much, went to Majka's party on Saturday, it was her thirteenth birthday, Mum bought her a kiddies' handbag, one of those you're meant to decorate yourself, you know the sort of shit.*

I don't write anymore, I just say that old dumbass, though what I think is: the dear old dumbass, my silly-billy.

In the morning my phone pings, a message from you vibrating under my cheek, as soft as rubber.

Good morning, my gorgeous puppy.

If I were a dog, I'd like someone to scratch me behind the ear, I'd like them to call me by a human name, to regularly change the water in my bowl; I'd like them to believe I haven't grown an inch and that I'm still a puppy that's only a few weeks old.

If I were a puppy, no one would care that I don't write anymore and that I just spread my legs. I'd have a zip instead of teeth and keep shedding hair, my owners would regularly brush me with a dog brush and have jumpers knitted from my hairs. That's what people do these days, Silvia showed me a video, *what a shame my dog is short-haired.*

Next time we meet, you raise your phone to your ear, *hello, Magda my dear!* Your voice turns into a syrupy sponge biscuit, you old dumbass, I stand there waiting for you to kiss me goodbye thinking about the word sponge, thinking about hunger. Beer sploshes around my stomach while you go *hello, Magda my dear*. I think of how the other night I watched you leave a pub, hand in hand with Magda. Magda drank nothing all night, she just sipped orange juice through a straw and she had no idea who I was.

I hope you understand how difficult this is for me, sweetheart, you say as you kiss me, old habits die hard, sometimes they cling to you like they're welded on, sometimes they throw themselves to the ground of their own accord, I wonder what dear Magda makes of this, *I hope you understand, sweetheart you're such a smart girl.*

55

Last year he spent his birthday with Tereza. She turned up, a doctor's note in one hand, a present in the other, wearing a coat on top of her dress but nothing underneath, having taken off her knickers in the lift with the hand holding his present, Ivan's two presents exchange glances. She turned up all smooth and cold like the jugs Ivan takes out of a hot kiln and sets down on the concrete to make the glazing crack, *if you don't do this step right it will look like it's ruined, you see, but if you take it straight out and leave it in the cold, it comes out even more beautiful.* She turned up with her fingernails freshly painted. That made Ivan happy, he couldn't stand it when she left bits of old varnish on her fingernails, *just look at yourself, Tereza, here's some remover, be a good girl and take it off.* Tereza rubs the remover onto her fingernails but gives him a dirty look as she does so, her short hair falling into her face. Ivan misses her long tresses, a rope for his hands, but Tereza has decided to chop it off, she didn't like to wear plaits because of her sticky-out ears. Ivan puts his hands behind her ears, tweaking them forward; Tereza blushes and grabs his hand, *stop that*, Tereza, the big girl who will soon leave school, who smokes Marlboro Reds and wants to discuss politics with him all the time, flapping her hands about and shouting *those fucking fascists* and when Ivan asks her how school is going, she says *oh, you know, sometimes I just lie in bed staring at the ceiling, like I switch off completely, I lie there feeling not really unhappy, just kind of nothingy.* She'd given him this expensive vinyl LP for his birthday last year, one he'd been looking for for ages, of course he wanted it and of course Tereza knew he did, Tereza just knows this kind of thing about him. After giving him the record she went to the bathroom to put on some make-up, red lipstick and thick black eyeliner, she also redid the nail varnish on her little toe as a bit had peeled off. This year, Ivan is spending his birthday underneath Magda. He's being straddled by Magda and her lace nightie, the nightie is brand new, whereas Magda is just freshly washed in Perwoll and in platinum blonde dye and shampoo that stops grey hair turning yellow although, as she informs him, in her case it's to stop platinum blonde hair turning yellow. And besides, Magda gets on with his daughter, they talk on the phone from time to time and call each other darling. Magda brings him lunch to work and strokes his hair as they go to sleep, with Magda everything is perfect, except for the erection which won't come, and how could it if Ivan is lying under Magda while, at the same time, he's on top of Tereza, he feels her all the time walking up and down under his pillow waiting for the right time to ring his doorbell. Ivan is tossing and turning but can't get comfortable with Tereza's elbows and head constantly poking him in the crown of his head.

17

In the pub, Silvia and I can't stop chatting away, *I just can't imagine being with someone else anymore, especially the sex, you know, the sex is so fucking good, cheers, but anyway, we were watching porn the other day, nothing weird about that, except he put on something with only women in it, so I said, hell, what's in this for me? He was, like really sweet about it though, he let me pick something else. Yeah, I know, I know, but I really can't imagine being with someone else anymore, once you've been with someone for so long you get, like used to it and don't care what kind of porn he watches, I know it's weird but then I'm weird too, and can you believe it, I had to tell him about incognito mode the other day, these old guys, they're hopeless you know, but that's beside the point, the point is that these days he like seems to be trying really hard to be a good boy, as my dad would say, he's being such a darling, so helpful all the time, but I don't know, if he got up to something now, you know, I think I'd dump him, I'd be the one to break up with him, that would be the last straw, and I think he knows that, he's like aware of that. And that's why he's being such a good boy, so that I should never have to leave him, although I don't know how long this can go on, I mean, like later in life, with him being his age and me being mine, how about another drink, becherovka or some other herbal shit, although last time I had some it made me puke, I can't really imagine drinking any more just now.*

Later that night I think about all the bullshit I said to Silvia and wonder what you've been up to, I have a headache and my mouth is dry, I'm pulling out one strand of hair after another, but the hair is sort of short, more like body hair.

But what really pisses me off is the fact that we don't really communicate, we never discuss anything, I don't feel like pretending anymore that everything is fine even if he doesn't answer my calls for days on end and then he rings like everything was just fine, hi, it's me, sweetheart, how have you been, sweetheart, feel like coming over and blowing me, sweetheart? Okay, don't laugh, he wouldn't put it that way, but you know what I mean, sometimes I don't even feel like picking up but at the same time I don't feel like starting a row, you know, I just want some peace and quiet, although I have no idea how long this can go on, I mean, like later in life and all that, and then there's all that stuff with my parents, pretending all along that they haven't a clue but I know they know, they've just given up or at least realised that if they did anything to him, that would be the end, I mean the end of things between them and me, I'm sure my dad would love to smash his face in but instead he just says he doesn't give a shit because I'll do whatever I want anyway and he's right, you know, I really love them very much now for knowing that I'll do whatever I want and I'd like to do something for them in return, shit, you've finished your drink already?

But anyway, I don't actually mind that we have to pretend we don't know each other, you know, when I see couples snogging in the street it makes me want to puke, I'd rather die than let someone shove their tongue down my throat in public.

But apart from that he's really been a good boy lately, doing just as he's told, he kept in touch even while his daughter was visiting, all right, he did say not to text him in the morning because that would look suspicious, I'm sure you remember that time I was at your place and your neighbour's cat caught a pigeon, God that was horrible, it tore the bird to shreds right before our eyes, the cat probably thought we can't catch our own, so it caught one for us, that was its way of showing it cared for us so, yeah, that's when Ivan told me to text later in the day, but that's okay, I don't have a problem with that. His daughter brought him this amazing fragrance, she manages a chain of perfume stores or something in Madrid, and this fragrance is just wow, it's something else, it smells like you've smeared honey all over yourself, in fact it says honey is one of the ingredients, she also brought him a bunch of samples, including some women's fragrances, he gave those to me, no use to him obviously, and his daughter asked him which one she should get for herself, but the one she's got him is the best, a proper aphrodisiac, the samples he's given me are also great but I can't really use them so I keep them hidden in a drawer at home along with all the other stuff I got from him, except for this candlestick he helped me make, that doesn't bother my parents because that was before they found out so it's still on the shelf with the vase you gave me on my birthday and all the shit I've brought back from London, Paris and the summer camps, otherwise I might totally forget that I've ever been anywhere apart from his place, but hey, that scent is totally the shit.

He's chilled out since I've been texting him later in the day, everything's great, I'm so happy, because things were, like really awful when his daughter was visiting, he might even have told her about his Magda or whatever her name was, but that's all history now, they're not together anymore, and we've never talked about it anyway but then again, when would he fit her in, seeing as he's with me all the time.

The other day I sent him a short story and he said he really liked it but why did it have so many dirty words, now tell me, is dick really a dirty word? I don't think so, and besides I didn't use it in that sense, it was simply a description, what else do you call it, penis sounds like urologist talk and prick, well, I used prick in the previous paragraph, you see what I mean, Silvia, synonyms, fuck, sorry to be so boring but now that we're on the subject, the same thing comes up in Esterházy, he's this Hungarian writer, a really hot guy actually but anyway, what I mean is it comes up in one of his books, not penises but fucking.

But tell you what, when you're in bed and want to be nice to him, how do you put it, you can't say what a lovely cock you've got, or oh your penis is so lovely, that's such a clinical term, but what else can you say?

Tell you what, diminutive words are the worst, they don't work at all, they're just a big no-no, it might make him think that you used a diminutive 'cause he has a small one when in fact all you wanted was to be affectionate!

Yeah, I know, and then you end up spouting some shit and then it all goes tits up, but if it actually makes you laugh, that could even be romantic.

Tell you what, another thing I find really annoying is when they don't say it straight out but say something like, stroke me, but what they really mean is their dick, because then it makes it sound as if the whole guy was just one megacock!

The next day I'm waiting for you in the patisserie, the becherovka didn't make me puke and I'm washing it down with some mineral water, the herbs bloom inside me, growing into my veins in the skin-covered hothouse, one that doesn't let in much light but a few butterflies still manage to flutter around anyway, like in the garden of the Natural History Museum, they settled right down on people, which frightens them, because it's a well-known fact that if a butterfly touches anyone, it dies, but these are so beautiful, the size of my palm.

At the next table a little girl is licking her ice cream and I find it offensive, shocking even, how looking at that little girl licking her ice cream turns me on. I feel ashamed of myself, tiny butterflies hatch inside me, settling on people who then fall to the ground one after the other and the staff of the Natural History Museum cover their bodies with white sheets. I know that you'd like my hair to be as blonde as this little girl's, or red, or black, any colour but my own boring brown. And you keep saying *I'd love you to wear your hair in a high ponytail,* as if you didn't hate my sticky-out ears, which are very obvious when my hair is up and yet you ask me to put it up anyway, that's love, that's butterflies.

You want me to wear a stay-on lipstick and a satin nightie but I only have a pair of jeans and a t-shirt from the market as I sit here waiting for you in this patisserie, where a little girl is licking ice cream like she's waiting for it to finally shoot its load.

And once it all falls apart, will it feel like when samples of expensive perfume wear off, or like a gas leak? That's the question, you dickheads!

His member is still warm from Tereza's hands but his feet are cold. He wanders around the flat, amongst the statues made by him and those made by his brothers who weren't his real brothers but they'd taken him to hospital when he cut his hand with a chisel, brought him a beer and comforted him by saying that though he may not be a great sculptor, he is certainly meticulous. They're good guys, except they didn't seem to realise that they've grown old and haven't produced anything worthwhile in years, and that their students lower their eyes when they listen to their advice, that the red carpet on which they make their entrance is only there because they've rolled it out themselves. Ivan is aware of all this and that's why he has no ambitions anymore, he has only his Tereza, he tells her that she's made all his dreams come true, which makes her happy and so she buys him presents which he has to hide in a drawer so his daughter and Magda don't see them. The only things he does wear are the t-shirts she's bought him, Tereza hugs him and whispers into his ear how great he looks in them, and when she's not whispering, Ivan rolls out his own red carpet, smoothes down its corners and runs his handheld vacuum cleaner over it, then he gets down on the floor and crawls towards her on his hands and knees, his feet are dreadfully cold but he keeps crawling, *Tereza, sweetheart.*

18

Now you really are being a good boy, as my dad would say. You go along with everything, like when I turn up at your place with a canvas and order you to *get up, we're going to paint*, I paint a vagina that looks wet although it's just glossy acrylic, and you paint a Celtic knot next to it. I paint a pair of buttocks red from a spanking, and you paint a heart next to it, you gaze at me for a long time the way you gaze at those pots and then say, *I could have got you pregnant a long time ago if I'd wanted to.*

For my birthday you've given me some latex knickers and face powder and a promise that you'll come to see me at the college because it's in another town where no one knows us, we can go for a coffee together, to the cinema, or play pool in the pub where they used to play songs by your favourite group, but I want you to come sober so we can get drunk together, you have to promise, because when you're tipsy I wonder why you even bothered, you just go on and on about the same old stuff I've been hearing again and again for years, when you've had a few drinks you say, *you're such a gorgeous little girl, you remind me of my daughter, you know*, and you make me put on the same song over and over again; and apart from the latex underwear and the promise, you've given me a jewellery box and announced proudly *I made this specially for you*, it's a jewellery box to keep all the pieces of jewellery you've given me over the years, none of which I can wear and all of which have been pregnant for a long time.

My back is walking through crowds of people and suddenly, through the see-through blouse, it hears *sweetheart!* That's you shouting at my back from the stairs, shouting through the crowds while I smile at you with my see-through mouth and my sweetiepie. So it was all worth it, worth washing my hair, washing my whole body and putting on the see-through blouse, it's all been worth it even though I originally planned to come naked to the exhibition opening so that you noticed me, but Silvia was right, all I needed to do was put on this see-through blouse. Then I got into Silvia's car, she put on some Danzig and we sat nodding our heads to the rhythm, but only gently so as not to exert ourselves too much and make my see-through blouse sweaty, at the exhibition opening we stood discreetly in the third row and then went out for a cigarette. As Silvia takes the pack from her pocket, I hear someone say *sweetheart!* I get goosebumps and strands of your hair on my sweetiepie and on my skin that's all chewed-up, and I turn around.

Is this your girlfriend, Ivan?

I tell you, Janík, you find a woman like this only once in a lifetime!

My see-through blouse has become even more see-through, it's coming apart at the shoulders and I have to pick it up from under the table. Silvia is smoking a joint outside the bar, Janík has made himself scarce, and you are stuffing your hands into my blouse, actually there's no need to stuff them in, they fit comfortably, there's plenty of room. When it's over we all get in the car, at a roundabout Silvia suddenly slams on the brakes, the safety belts hold our bodies firm, mine is see-through, so only just.

At Silvia's I sit in your lap and you make me play the same track over and over, *this is the best drummer ever,* but I don't mind, *and you're the loveliest little girl on the planet,* Silvia is twirling her glass round by the stem, *so this guy was from Egypt, he had the biggest cock I've ever seen, but otherwise there was no picture or sound, so I wouldn't be seen dead with an Egyptian again.* Later we spend a long time lying on Sylvia's parents' bed. I tell you that I'm ovulating and that when I was in London I went to the Natural History Museum with my cousin and there was this hothouse with butterflies flying all around us and settling on our hands, some were as big as my face, some were see-through like my blouse, and there they were, hatching in the glass cases before our very eyes.

My cousin was thirteen at the time, with lovely fair hair and full lips. I hope she doesn't settle on anyone too soon, and even if she does, I hope that their touch doesn't count, that she won't die by the morning like a butterfly, perhaps not every touch is fatal. When I was in England you wrote to me every day *come back home, sweetheart*, and then you settled on me and came back to life.

You settled on me and stuck your cock in my mouth, it's not the biggest cock on the planet, but oh that picture, that sound, *sweetheart*.

Tereza, sweetheart, I'm past it, what's all this got to do with me, you said then, and didn't go off to vote.

So we're lying in Silvia's parents' bed. I tell you I'm ovulating, like I tell you all sorts of things, with you I can jabber non-stop, I tell you that my grandpa's house was the most beautiful and most cherished in Radnovce because my grandpa's parents used to be landed gentry and the house was taken to the open air village museum, are you even listening to me? Of course I'm listening, with every fibre of my body, and all I can think about is wanting to take you away, like that most beautiful and most cherished house, and about where I'm going to put your last brick, about how I will turn you to face east so that the sun shines in my eyes whenever I come to look at you, press my face to your wall, hear your door squeal, and listen to people hanging around your gate.

What was that you were saying, sweetheart?

What was I was saying, yeah, I was saying that art is only any good with you, that's when it's best, the most cherished, because love is something we don't speak about, the only thing that's allowed is lying in bed, we just have to lie there, as smooth as little children, everything has got to be smooth, you're smooth too, the clock is ticking smoothly and the wine slides down my throat smoothly, even though it's trying to scramble back up as I speak, the lift glides up slowly and smoothly and I don't bump into anyone who might give me away, and even if I did bump into someone, as happened once with my aunt, they would just look the other way and even if they did keep looking, they couldn't see that I'm not wearing knickers. So we don't speak about love, God forbid that I should say I love you, God forbid that I suggest we go out for a beer together, just to the pub around the corner, the one with all the drunks and endless live football; moaning is allowed, smooth gliding and sliding in is allowed, but not a word about love or stuff to do with the future, or politics, or the past, or feminism, or the books that I've read but you haven't, or meetings with writers you're jealous of, or the boys you know nothing about, none of that is allowed, and yet it crowds onto my tongue as it presses against your cock, like a teeny-weeny, simple childish thought. It crowds and presses, because I happen to be ovulating and when we kissed I could feel the bald spot on your head, it was smooth but we don't talk about that either.

At midnight you take a taxi home, I go to lie down next to Silvia in her room, but Silvia is already asleep, some wine spit dribbling from her mouth. The next day I ring you and get *the number you have dialled is currently unavailable....*

I wish you many happy years together, Janík said. And after everyone was gone, you stuffed your hands everywhere, under my empty blouse, under my empty skin, into my empty head, while Silvia left the bar to light up a joint, casually, outside, in the square by the roundabout, with everyone watching, later we lay in her parents' bed and after that I don't know because I have no idea where you are, for days there's been only emptiness where you were, only your hands still squatting inside my head.

I don't write anymore, I just spread my legs even when I'm ovulating. I'm an ordinary little girl, I go to school, I get top marks, but just for myself, as my parents no longer care. So I always bring home top marks and in the evening before every test I flop down on a bench, cigarette in hand, moaning about being fed up with studying and all the assignments, what's the point of parsing sentences anyway, I hang around cafés where men leer at me and when my dad rings and says, *I just wanted to hear your voice, my pet,* and then *where have you been mooching about,* I get worked up, what does he mean, mooching about? And in PE a twelve-minute run makes me as sweaty as all my classmates, I also sweat in the lift, whether or not I'm wearing knickers, and although I still go to the library to borrow Esterházy because his *Harmonia caelestis* is out of print, I also go to the Cinemax to watch a costume drama with a female lead who is too headstrong for the men of her times and I refuse to feel bad about it, well, okay, just a little, and on Sundays, when I'm back at the halls of residence, I gossip with my mates and we share the food we've brought from home, *have some of my meatloaf, I'd rather have some of your schnitzel,* and then in the showers we eye up each other's bums and pubes and everyone's sad because I don't have a flat tummy like Klaudia and Klaudia doesn't have tits like I do; I'm saving my prettiest knickers for Fridays when I go to see you, the rest of the time I wear cotton ones even when I'm not on my period; so, anyway, I really don't know why you say *you're amazing, sweetheart, the most beautiful girl on the planet,* now that I don't write anymore, or do anything.

You say *you're amazing, sweetheart, the most beautiful girl on the planet,* but then you also say *you're not right in the head, leave me alone, stop hounding me, you keep ringing, so no wonder I switch my phone off, what with your constant ringing, if I don't answer it means I can't,* and you also say, *come on, what's the big deal, I just didn't pick up, I don't have my mobile on me when I'm in the shower,* but you also used to say, *why did you ring, I was in the shower with Magda,* although you didn't say where Magda is now, instead you said, *you're amazing, sweetheart, the most beautiful girl on the planet, your lips swell up after orgasm, please don't write about us anymore, what if someone reads it.*

Your hands are squatting inside my head; squatting there taking a shit.

I've given up trying to reach you by phone, I'm resigned to waiting devotedly and as I wait I suddenly remember how, years ago, I told you that when I grew up I wanted a husband like my grandpa or Péter Esterházy. I still fancy a man like that, I'd pick his grey hairs from my black jumper, black trousers, black suspenders, black knickers and red thighs. I still want a husband like Péter Esterházy, but I also fancy a sculptor and a painter and an environmental activist, I'd like a man I'll have to kiss first because he'll be too shy, and also one who will give me one orgasm after another, I'd also like a nerdy one with glasses who everyone makes fun of for his thin and greasy hair, and also one that jabbers non-stop. I fancy a singer in a hard rock band, but also a jazz singer and a singer from Pink Floyd, preferably both at the same time, and I'd also like a drummer and a man with a thick head of hair who owns a tea room, and a teacher whose head is as bald as a coot, like Rumoš when he was in the sanatorium, I'd like a man who's symmetrical as well as one with a crooked nose, though not a crooked cock, God forbid, and I'd also like a man who likes reading as well as cooking, and I'd like to count up how many of those men are you, I've started totting them up and just then my mobile rings, *sweetheart.*

I'd like a man I can kiss from top to toe. One I love so much that I could eat him whole. One who leaps into my mouth of his own accord. Who will lick me clean from the inside and kiss my bleeding body better every month. If I could eat you, I'd douse you in oil and smear you with lard, which perhaps I'd make from my own fat. But all I can do with you is put you in my mouth, you're impossible to chew up, you make my jaw cramp and you scratch my throat. If I were able to eat you, I'd have been carrying you in my belly long ago, upside down.

I'd like a man who would make sense from head to toe.

I'd like a man to whom I could keep telling I love you over and over, stopping only when I run out of breath, then I'd take a deep breath and continue.

I have eaten boys who could be kissed from top to bottom, from head to toe, I've eaten everyone who let me, and now I roll around town like a piece of brawn waiting to be sliced, I could have eaten up my teachers too, in fact I have done. I've told them I don't have any work to hand in, *I've been going through a rough patch, miss*, and the teacher strokes my back, *my sister knows a good psychiatrist, do you want me to make an appointment for you, Tereza?* I was rude to another teacher, I walked out of his class and went back later to apologise, but he said he was here for us rather than the other way round, and I cried because he was so hot, he might have been a drummer or a saxophone player when he was young, *I've been going through a rough patch, sir.*

He laughed and said, *I bet there's a young man involved,* and I laughed along with him.

The only things that are really funny are those that are true at the same time, when I'm with you I laugh but back at home tears spring into my mouth of their own accord, they say, *we're going through a rough patch*.

My phone rings and you say, *sweetheart*, and I want to say, *I respect you, you know, but you don't respect me, even if sometimes you say I'm all you want, so that's where we're at, you and me,* and also, *I've been waiting for you for days, my dad keeps telling me I ought to have more patience, so I waited and waited, I did nothing, I didn't write or spread my legs,* and also *let me tell you something you may find interesting, I slept with Anita once, we did it in the showers in halls, she hadn't shaved anywhere and the whole thing was wonderful, so feminine, and I felt self-conscious being so smooth, and the wet shower curtain kept getting stuck to my bum,* and I'm sure you'd say *Tereza, you're not right in the head,* but instead you say, *are you coming, sweetheart, come over, I'll take you from behind.*

I'm lying under you and hear your stomach rumbling, there are insects fluttering around in it, fruit flies, bluebottles, butterflies, they're all in there, their little wings touching, they barely have room to move.

I want to tell you *I wish you lived inside me like inside a whale even though I've lost a lot of weight, do you like my legs, darling,* but you suddenly get up without saying a word, put your boxers on, put on first one sock, then the other, then your trousers and your shirt, which you button right up to your neck, and go to the kitchen, I hear the lighter click. I want to say, *what's up, darling,* but I can hardly go stark naked as I am, I glance down at my body and see insects flitting about, flies mostly.

I don't know what's happened, Silvia, everything was great, fantastic, then we lay there next to each other and I thought this was just a pause and we would continue.

I thought you'd pour me another drink, you were in such a good mood when I arrived, the glasses were laid out in the bedroom, but you also drank from my breasts, one for the road.

But then, all of a sudden, he gets dressed, lights a cigarette and looks dead serious, so I just don't know what to make of it, I feel horrible, you know what I mean, it makes me feel ugly when one minute the man is lying beside me and the next, all of a sudden, he gets up and acts like he doesn't know me, as if he has nothing to do with me, so what's going to happen now? What will I do if, when I straddle you like I did the goat, it feels like something is pressing between my legs and squeezing the butterflies out of my belly, I'll pull them out of my mouth one by one along with the strands of hair. You'll try ringing me every day until I finally pick up, you'll take a deep breath through your tears and go

IloveyouIloveIloveyou until you run out of breath and collapse in a heap. And then I'll reach into my mouth again and what crawls out of it is a strand of hair that I swallowed a long time ago, no longer grey, or amazing, or post-orgasmically swollen, it'll be just an ordinary strand of brown hair that I pull out of my mouth, with a stranger's hand dangling from it, I can't even begin to imagine such a thing.

It's a long time since I was thirteen, Silvia, this isn't fun anymore, but how could it possibly be otherwise? Who else would want me, who else would understand me, I can't imagine what it would be like without him, and yet, he just went and got up, out of the blue, got dressed and said it was impossible for him to love me, I can't tell you how I hate it when he goes on about that, I don't think this is fun anymore, but how could things possibly be otherwise?

Julia Sherwood is a translator (with Peter Sherwood) from Slovak, Czech, Polish, Russian and German into English as well as into Slovak. Now based in London, she was born and grew up in Bratislava, Slovakia, and studied English and Slavonic languages and literature in Cologne, London and Munich.

Peter Sherwood is a translator and scholar. He taught at the School of Slavonic and East European Studies, University College London from 1972 to 2007 and University of North Carolina, Chapel Hill, from 2008 to 2014.

Parthian, Cardigan SA43 1ED
www.parthianbooks.com
Published by Parthian in 2025
© Nicol Hochholczerová, 2023 Original edition published by KK Bagala, Levice, Slovakia, 2021 as Táto izba sa nedá zjesť
Translation © Julia and Peter Sherwood, 2024
Print ISBN 978-1-917140-41-6
Ebook ISBN 978-1-917140-42-3
Editor: Gwen Davies
Typeset by Syncopated Pandemonium
Printed by 4edge
Published with the financial support of the Books Council of Wales
A cataloguing record for this book is available from the British Library. This book is published with the financial support of the SLOLIA Board, Slovak Literary Centre